How NOT to Marry a Princess

Written by Jan Burchett and Sara Vogler

Illustrated by Dusan Pavlic

Collins

Chapter 1

Are you a prince who wants to get married? Is your father trying to find you a bride? Is he reaching for a book called *How to Marry a Princess*? Tell him to put it back on the shelf immediately. THAT BOOK IS DANGEROUS!

Let me explain. My name is Ethelbert Goodfellow and I am Royal Chamberlain to King Malingo. But not for much longer. I fear I'm going to lose my job very soon. It all started when King Malingo declared it was time that his son, Prince Wilbur, married a princess.

Poor Wilbur. He just wants to live happily ever after with Gertrude, the gardener, and grow turnips. But King Malingo won't hear of it. He threw *How to Marry a Princess* at me and told me I must help Wilbur find a royal bride or else.

He said the book was full of good ideas. Well, it's full of ideas that sound good. But believe me, it should be called *How NOT to Marry a Princess*. Have a look inside this dreadful book at the ideas that Wilbur and I tried. You will see from all the notes that they don't work.

Chapter 2

The princess and the pea test

You will need:

a princess

a pea

100 mattresses

Do the following:

1. Invite the princess to stay at the palace for the night.

2. Make up a bed with 100 mattresses.

3. Put a pea under the bottom mattress.

4. If the princess can feel the pea through all the mattresses, she's a real princess and you can marry her.

Notes
Don't try this at home! The first princess couldn't climb the mountain of mattresses, the second one ate the pea, and poor Princess Pansy got catapulted out of the window.
Ethelbert Goodfellow (Royal Chamberlain)
PS Mattresses are very heavy!

Notes

It was very hard to find 100 mattresses. I had to hand mine over and sleep on my hard bedroom floor!

Wilbur (Prince)

Ethelbert clearly chose the wrong sort of princess. He should have looked in the royal address book.

Malingo (King)

Note found pinned to the castle drawbridge –

WARNING

Beware of dangerous mattresses

Pansy (Princess/mattress pilot)

Rescue a sleeping princess

You will need:

a princess asleep
in a castle

a thorny forest
surrounding
the castle

a trusty sword

Do the following:

1. Hack through the thorny forest with your trusty sword.

2. Wake the princess.

3. Rescue the princess.

4. Marry the princess.

Notes

This idea is rubbish. Thorny forests are very hard to hack through. By the time Wilbur got to the castle, Princess Poppy had woken up, cut her own way out and gone home. It might have been quicker if Wilbur hadn't taken a <u>rusty</u> sword instead of a trusty one.

Ethelbert Goodfellow (Royal Chamberlain)

It wasn't my fault. It's not easy to read instructions with your father shouting in your ear! Gertrude never shouts in my ear. She just shows me how to plant turnips.

Wilbur (Prince)

I hope you can still help me with the turnips when you're married, Wilbur.

I NEVER SHOUT!

Malingo (King)

How long does it take to cut through a forest and rescue a princess? I'm off. Don't bother to get in touch!

Poppy (Princess)

Chapter 4

The frog prince test

You will need:

a princess

a pond

a frog spell

Do the following:

1. Use the frog spell to turn yourself into a frog.

2. Hop into the pond.

3. Wait for the princess to walk round the pond.

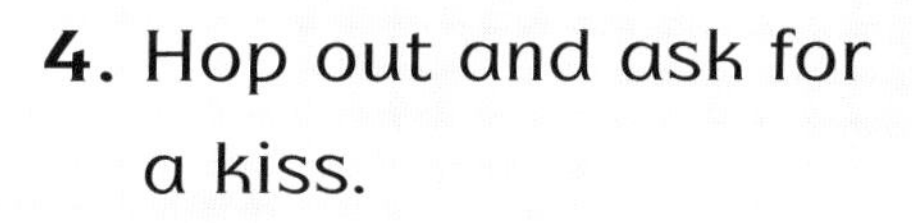

4. Hop out and ask for a kiss.

5. If she is a real princess, the kiss will turn you back into a prince and you can marry her.

Notes

No good! Frog Wilbur got stuck in the mud. We had to scoop him out with a bucket. Princess Primrose was so disgusted by frogs she climbed a tree. She was rescued by another princess.

Ethelbert Goodfellow (Royal Chamberlain)

Notes

I nearly drowned! Gertrude wouldn't have made me hop into a pond. She says pond water is for watering turnips.

Wilbur (Prince)

Ethelbert must have used the wrong spell. It took three days for Wilbur to turn back into a prince and his ears are still green.

Malingo (King)

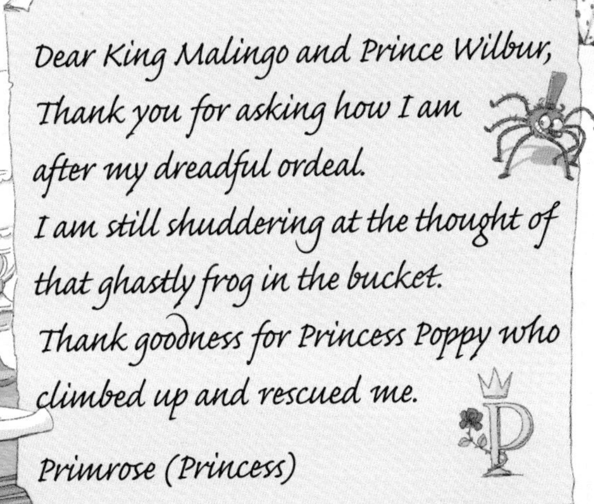

Dear King Malingo and Prince Wilbur,

Thank you for asking how I am after my dreadful ordeal.

I am still shuddering at the thought of that ghastly frog in the bucket.

Thank goodness for Princess Poppy who climbed up and rescued me.

Primrose (Princess)

Chapter 5

Rescue a princess from a dragon

You will need:

a dragon

a princess

a high tower

Do the following:

1. Lock the princess in the tower.

2. Put the dragon at the bottom of the tower.

3. Scare the dragon away.

4. Rescue the princess.

5. Marry the princess.

Notes

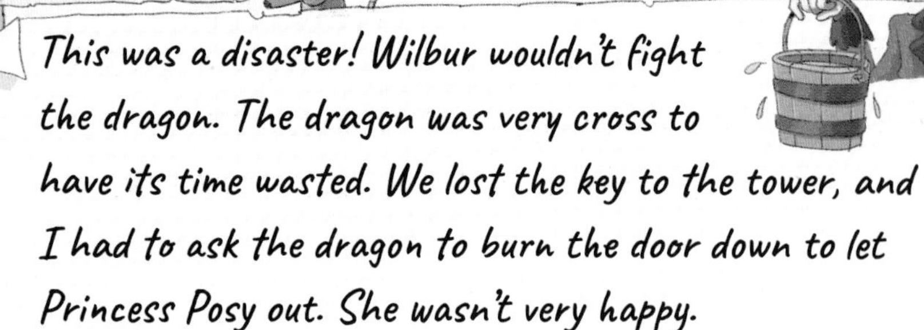

This was a disaster! Wilbur wouldn't fight the dragon. The dragon was very cross to have its time wasted. We lost the key to the tower, and I had to ask the dragon to burn the door down to let Princess Posy out. She wasn't very happy.

Ethelbert Goodfellow (Royal Chamberlain)

Notes

I wanted to try a different tactic – I thought I'd try to negotiate with the dragon instead of fighting, but it got in such a huff. Thankfully, Gertrude understands me. She gave me turnip soup.
Wilbur (Prince)

I am furious. Wilbur is still not married. Ethelbert has been completely useless. I am going to lock him in the tower. After I've had a new door put on.
Malingo (King)

What a waste of my time. On the plus side, Dragon and I have become great friends and are hosting a bonfire party next week.

Posy (Princess)

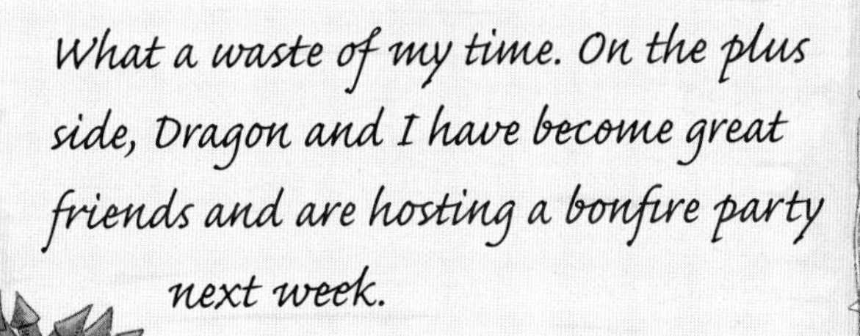

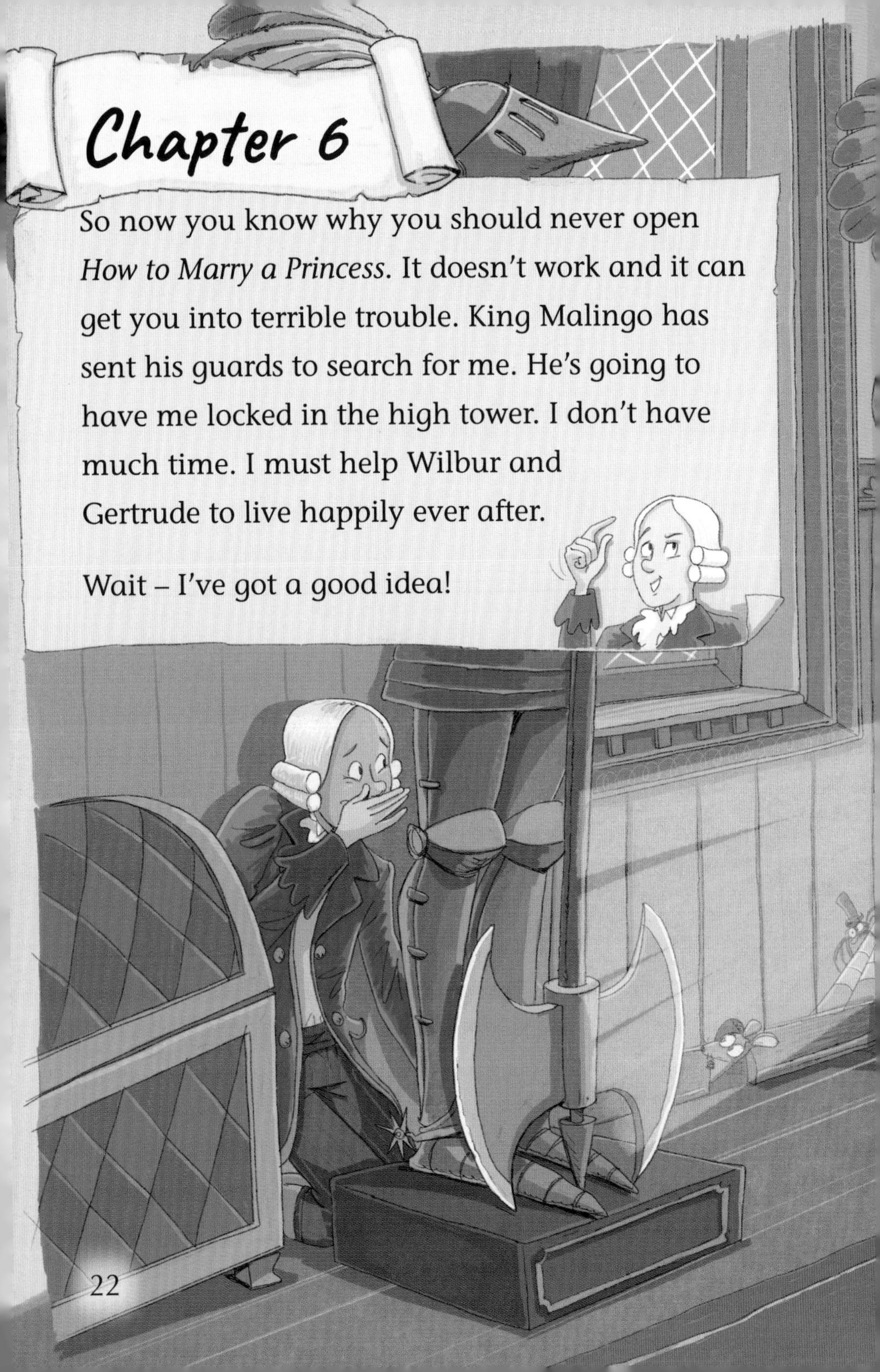

Chapter 6

So now you know why you should never open *How to Marry a Princess*. It doesn't work and it can get you into terrible trouble. King Malingo has sent his guards to search for me. He's going to have me locked in the high tower. I don't have much time. I must help Wilbur and Gertrude to live happily ever after.

Wait – I've got a good idea!

Ethelbert Goodfellow's Good Idea

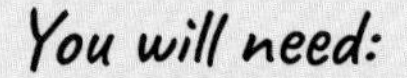

You will need:

- Prince Wilbur
- Gertrude the gardener
- a pumpkin
- two white mice
- a magic wand

Do the following:

1. Change the pumpkin into a coach.
2. Change the white mice into horses.
3. Put Prince Wilbur and Gertrude in the coach.
4. Tell them to run away together.
5. Hope they live happily ever after.

Notes

It worked – for Prince Wilbur and Gertrude.

Chapter 7

Dear Ethelbert,
Thank you for your help. I'm the happiest prince in the world now I'm with Gertrude. It's very mean of Father to lock you in that high tower. Don't despair. Gertrude and I have a plan (enclosed). I drew the pictures as well.
Wilbur (Prince)

Prince Wilbur and Gertrude's Rescue Plan

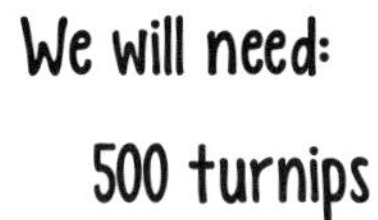

We will need:

500 turnips

strong glue

a saw

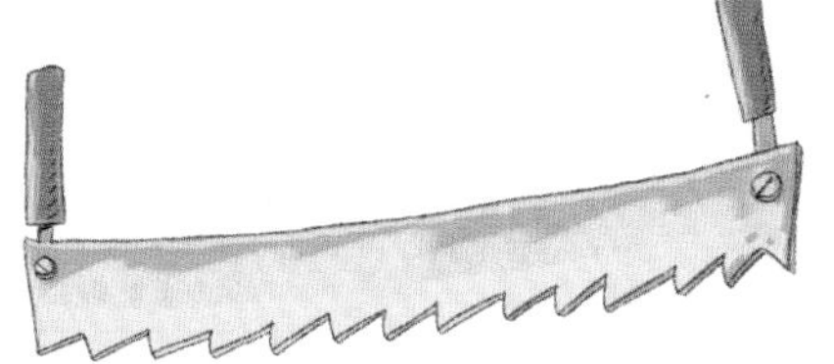

This is what we're going to do:

1. Stick the turnips together to make a turnip ladder.
2. Climb up the tower.
3. Saw through the window bars.
4. Free the prisoner.

Oh dear. Wilbur and Gertrude's plan isn't going to work. No one can make a turnip ladder.

Wait a minute. A turnip ladder has just slapped against my window!

I'm free! Prince Wilbur and Gertrude's plan worked perfectly, although a goat tried to eat the turnip ladder while I was climbing down. King Malingo was furious, but I don't care. I'm Royal Chamberlain to Prince Wilbur and Gertrude now. They have a wonderful palace and vegetable patch, and there's no sign of *How to Marry a Princess* anywhere. We're all going to live happily ever after.

Princess adventures

Ideas for reading

Written by Gill Matthews
Primary Literacy Consultant

Reading objectives:

- understand both the books that they can already read accurately and fluently and those that they listen to by:
- drawing on what they already know or on background information and vocabulary provided by the teacher
- answering and asking questions

Spoken language objectives:

- ask relevant questions to extend their understanding and knowledge
- use relevant strategies to build their vocabulary
- use spoken language to develop understanding through speculating, hypothesising, imagining and exploring ideas

Curriculum links: Relationships education – Caring friendships

Word count: 1240

Interest words: disgusted, shuddering, ghastly

Build a context for reading

- Ask children to look closely at the front cover. Discuss the figures they can see.
- Demonstrate how to read the title, emphasising the word *Not*. Ask what the title means to them.
- Read the back-cover blurb. Explore children's knowledge of fairy tales, discussing typical characters, storylines and outcomes.
- Ask how they think a modern fairy tale might be different from a traditional fairy tale.

Understand and apply reading strategies

- Read pp2–5 aloud to the children using punctuation and meaning to help you to read with appropriate expression. To check their understanding, ask children to explain what this first chapter is about.
- Read pp6–9 aloud. Ask children which fairy tale is referred to on pp6–7. Discuss the problems with the plan in order to check their understanding of the notes on pp8–9.